BAND GEEKS

Dude, Where's My Saxophone?

Calico
An Imprint of Magic Wagon
www.abdopublishing.com

by Amy Cobb
Illustrated by Anna Cattish

Lo

You

om an

t Cade

on Bl

www.abdopublishing.com

Published by Magic Wagon, a division of ABDO,
PO Box 398166, Minneapolis, Minnesota 55439.
Copyright © 2015 by Abdo Consulting Group, Inc.
International copyrights reserved in all countries. No part of this
book may be reproduced in any form without written permission from
the publisher. Calico™ is a trademark and logo of Magic Wagon.

Printed in the United States of America, North Mankato, Minnesota.
102014
012015

 **THIS BOOK CONTAINS
RECYCLED MATERIALS**

Written by Amy Cobb
Illustrations by Anna Cattish
Edited by Heidi M.D. Elston, Megan M. Gunderson & Bridget O'Brien
Cover and interior design by Candice Keimig

Library of Congress Cataloging-in-Publication Data

Cobb, Amy, author.
  Dude, where's my saxophone? / by Amy Cobb ; illustrated by Anna
Cattish.
    pages cm. -- (Band geeks)
  Summary: The whole Benton Bluff Junior High band is at band camp,
and when things start to go missing everybody blames Zac, the class
clown--but when Zac's saxophone disappears he suspects that it is
someone in another group trying to sabotage Benton Bluff, and sets
out to uncover the culprit.
  ISBN 978-1-62402-073-5
  1. Music camps--Juvenile fiction. 2. Bands (Music)--Juvenile fiction.
3. Theft--Juvenile fiction. 4. Competition (Psychology)--Juvenile
fiction. 5. Junior high schools--Juvenile fiction. [1. Music camps--
Fiction. 2. Camps--Fiction. 3. Bands (Music)--Fiction. 4. Stealing--
Fiction. 5. Competition (Psychology)--Fiction. 6. Junior high schools--
Fiction. 7. Schools--Fiction.] I. Cattish, Anna, illustrator. II. Title.
  PZ7.1.C63Du 2015
  813.6--dc23
                                          2014035975

With extra special thanks to Larry Vaught for graciously
sharing his expertise and passion for music.
I am forever grateful to Clelia Gore, Megan Gunderson,
and Candice Keimig for taking a chance on me. —AC

TABLE OF CONTENTS

Chapter 1
WANNA BET?

Davis Beadle beat his drumsticks on the back of the bus seat I shared with Sherman Frye. Sherman read wildflower facts out loud from this field guide he'd brought. Nonstop. For two hours. My brain was in total snooze mode.

Finally, gravel crunched under our tires and we rolled to a stop beneath a giant oak tree. We were here! So were a ton of other kids, already lugging around instruments and settling into cabins.

"Band camp!" I pumped my fists in the air. Then I scrambled across Sherman and hopped out of my seat. "Five days of nonstop fun, here I come!"

"Sit down, Zac." Mr. Byrd, our school band director, stood in the aisle. He pushed his glasses up on his nose and said, "Let's chat first."

"May as well get comfortable." I kicked back in my seat, propping an elbow on Sherman's head. Sherman laughed. But Byrd frowned. "Just kidding, sir," I said. But I sort of wasn't. I mean, the whole band knows Byrd's "chats" are more like twenty-minute lectures.

"Anyway, we are here to have fun, as Zac said," Mr. Byrd began. "But we're also here to grow as musicians. Everyone should do his or her best. Behave as well as you do each day in the band room." His eyes locked on mine. "Or even better."

"Man, you just KO'd my plans." I faked a one-two punch. "Total knockout."

"I mean it, Zac. Cut the goofing off," he said.

Byrd probably secretly wanted to have fun, too. But once he became a teacher? *Poof!* His sense of humor disappeared. That was my theory, anyway.

"Now, take your instrument off the bus with you," Mr. Byrd continued, eyeing me. "This means neck strap, mouthpiece, reeds. Everything."

Tally Nguyen smiled from across the aisle. "Yeah, Zac."

I play saxophone in the Benton Bluff Junior High band. And I forget all of that stuff for practice sometimes. Okay, a lot. Sue me.

Byrd clapped his hands then. "Let's go register. File in, everyone."

Byrd led the way off the bus and out into the sunshine. We followed behind him, like junior high band soldiers. Byrd acted like a drill sergeant most of the time. He even insisted we call him sir.

But Byrd sure didn't dress like a drill sergeant. He looked ready to hit the beach instead. Today, brightly colored huts dotted his tropical shirt. He paired blue shorts with flip-flops and tube socks, which stretched tight around his calves. His leg hair curled over the top, like a bazillion tiny, fuzzy spiders trying to escape from the elastic.

So everyone sort of hung around outside the camp office, waiting for cabin assignments. And while Byrd checked in our band, I checked out the girls in the other bands.

"She's cute." I elbowed Sherman when a girl carrying a trumpet case walked past.

"What about Baylor?" Sherman asked.

"Baylor's cute, too." Baylor Meece is one of the nicest girls in our band, too. "But we're just friends."

Sherman's eyebrows wiggled up and down. "You sure?"

"Maybe." Baylor smiled at me a lot. So sometimes it was hard to tell.

"I prefer other flute players," Sherman went on.

"I like girls who play woodwinds, too," I said. "And girls who play brass. And percussion."

Sherman blinked. "That's all the girls, Zac."

"Yep." I grinned. "I know. And right now, I'm gonna get to know her." I rushed toward the girl with the trumpet.

"Wait! I'm coming too." He ran to catch up.

"Fine," I said. "But act cool."

Sherman isn't exactly the coolest geek in the band. More like the weirdest. He keeps a yo-yo tucked in his pocket and is always showing off his newest trick. And he warms up every day before band practice. Like, seriously warms up, with jumping jacks and yoga. Super weird. But I still like hanging out with him. Most of the time.

"Act cool." Sherman nodded, his brown curls bobbing up and down. "Got it."

"Hey, watch this." I stooped to pick a flower with bright yellow petals. "I'm gonna give her this daisy."

Sherman held up his wildflower field guide. "Actually, that's a black-eyed Susan. See how the center is brown? Daisies have yellow centers with white petals."

"Dude, who cares? It's summer break."

But I didn't give Sherman time to answer. I hurried on over to the girl with the trumpet. "A flower for you," I said, holding it out to her.

Her eyes widened, but she took it. "It's pretty," she said. "Thanks."

"You're welcome." I smiled. "My name's Zac Wiles, by the way. What's yours?"

"Aubrey Fowler."

"Hey," Sherman jumped in, "if you mixed the letters around, that would spell flower."

Aubrey laughed and tucked the flower I gave her behind one ear.

"Nice," I said.

"Did you know that's a black-eyed Susan?" Sherman asked her.

Aubrey shook her head.

"Yep," Sherman said. "It's sad so many earthlings don't know the different species of wildflowers."

"*Sherman*," I said, hoping he'd zip it.

But he ignored me and kept on going. "Wildflowers are important, you know? I wish we could petition the president to create a law so we could learn more about them in school."

"Great idea." Aubrey nodded.

"Hey, Sherman. I think I just saw a . . ." I tried to think of a flower he'd told me about on the bus. "A chocolate lily!" I remembered it because, hello, chocolate. And because Lilly Reyes plays flute in our band. "Maybe you should check it out."

"Impossible!" Sherman said.

"Dude!" I wiped my cheek with the back of my hand. "You just spit a little."

"Sorry!" Sherman dabbed at my cheek, too.

"Dude, I got it," I said, pushing his hand away.

That stopped him. There was no stopping Sherman about this wildflower stuff, though. "Anyway, you couldn't have seen a chocolate lily, Zac." He flipped open his guidebook. "See? Page 16 shows their range. They don't grow around here."

"Okay, Sherman. I get it." Then I shot him a "You're killing me here!" look. But Aubrey was digging this wildflower stuff, too. She obviously liked geeky guys. I didn't stand a chance.

By then some other kids had gathered around anyway. This one guy lugging a sax case said, "Do pansies grow here?" He laughed. "'Cause you both look like pansies to me!"

"Nate Lutz! That was mean," Aubrey said.

"What?" Nate acted surprised. Then he looked at me. "Check out all the camouflage this kid's wearing. Dude, I can still see you."

"Real original," I said. I always wear camouflage, so I'd heard that lame joke before. I made a big show of rolling my eyes before totally changing the subject. "What band are you in, Aubrey?"

"Morrison Junior High," she said. "What about you?"

"Benton Bluff Junior High. And hey, I'm not bragging or anything," I grinned, "but my sax skills are pretty cool."

"Puh-lease!" Nate nodded toward his sax case. "Nobody's better than me. I make the all-stars camp band every year."

"Yeah, Benton Bluff's a bunch of losers," the kid beside Nate said. His spiky hair reminded me of the pine needles all around us. He held a sax case, too. "Check out their director. What a goober!"

"Ethan!" Aubrey said.

Sherman tapped on my shoulder. "We should probably go now."

But I wasn't ready to go. Not yet. I mean, maybe I goof off a lot, but I didn't like these kids making fun of our band. Or talking about Mr. Byrd, either.

Byrd is my favorite teacher, even if he does act all tough. See, I already have Byrd figured out. That act is just to keep us in line. He's an ex–band geek. He still loves band and all of the kids in band, too.

"We're no losers," I said. "And you just wish you had Mr. Byrd."

"No way," Ethan said. "Mrs. Hendrix is our band director. She directs the best band in the state. Us!"

"Ask the governor who's best," I set him straight. "We won a competition to play at his mansion."

"Big whoop!" Nate said. "We didn't enter that competition, or we'd have won. But we'll prove we're the best when we beat you at Sound Off."

Sound Off is an annual band camp competition. Every day, each band gets points for different things. I don't even know for what. I've never really cared before. But I do know on the last day of camp, the band with the most points takes home a trophy.

Then Nate made a big show of wiping fake tears from his eyes. "Your band'll go home crying."

"No we won't," I said. "'Cause we wouldn't want to get tears on our new trophy."

"Your band win the trophy? Ha!" Nate said. "Wanna bet on it?" Then he reached into his pocket and pulled out a ten-dollar bill. "This says we'll win."

"Seriously?" I asked.

Nate laughed. "Unless you're too chicken."

"Bawk! Bawk!" Ethan flapped his arms like wings.

I thought about it. I didn't want to bet money. But I was no chicken, either. "Taking your money when we win doesn't seem fair," I finally said.

Nate shoved it back in his pocket. "Then you name the bet."

"I dunno. Maybe whoever loses has to dress up like his band director on the last day at Sound Off."

"You're on," Nate said. "I can't wait to see you in your director's straw hat and goofy shirt."

"Nah, you better pucker up. Because you'll be wearing bright pink lipstick, just like your director."

"Zac!" Sherman said, tugging on my arm. "Let's go. Mr. Byrd's looking for us."

"I'm not worried about Byrd." I shrugged Sherman off, playing it cool. But I kind of was. I mean, I didn't want Byrd all mad at me on our first day here. So then I said, "See you around, Aubrey Fowler. And I'll see you boys when our band wins the Sound Off trophy." I looked at Nate. "You'll look sharp in your band director's high heels."

Nate rolled his eyes. "Whatever. Later, losers."

Yeah, last year I'd been more worried about having fun than winning Sound Off. In fact, I wasn't even sure what we had to do to get points. But after what Nate and Ethan had said, I planned to find out. Our band would rack up more points than theirs. No joke!

Chapter 2
BUNKING WITH BYRD

After that, Sherman and I headed back to the camp office. Byrd was standing outside with the rest of the band, holding a clipboard.

"Boys, where have you been?" he asked, without giving us time to answer. "Unless it's designated free time, please stick together. It's unfair for the rest of the band to wait for you. Understand?"

"Yes, sir," Sherman said.

"Zac?" Mr. Byrd said.

I nodded. "Yes, sir."

"Good. Now, I have some important information to share with you all." Then Byrd sort of mumbled to himself as he flipped through the sheets clipped to his board. "Camp map. Camper conduct rules. Daily menu. Sound Off points."

"Hey, what do we gotta do to get a bunch of Sound Off points?" I asked.

Byrd looked at me over the top of his glasses. "I'm surprised you asked that, Zac."

Of course he was. I mean, I'd never asked about getting more points before. I'd never cared. But if we were going to beat Morrison, I needed to know.

"However," Mr. Byrd continued, "our band isn't focusing on points. Instead, strive to do your best, as individuals and as a group. Okay?"

"Okay," I said. But really, I planned to leave that "do your best" stuff to the rest of the band, while I figured out how to get us more points. They could all thank me later.

"What are we doing next, Mr. Byrd?" Baylor asked. She always asks a ton of questions. Besides playing clarinet, she reports news for our school paper, the *Benton Bluff Bloodhound*.

Byrd flipped to one of the pages. "Here's our schedule. First, we'll have a group welcome for all bands, followed by a camp staff meet and greet. Then we have band rehearsal."

"Just us?" Baylor interrupted.

Mr. Byrd nodded.

That's one of the cool things about this camp. Sometimes we practice with just our band. At least, the people who didn't already have summer plans and were able to come. And sometimes, all the bands here play together to make one giant band.

"Before supper, you'll choose two electives," Mr. Byrd went on. "This year, there's music theory, introduction to jazz, and beginner marching."

Sherman started marching in place. "Sign me up for that!"

"Hold on." Mr. Byrd held up one hand. "There are all-stars one-on-one instrument workshops, too. At the end of camp, judges will choose the top instrumentalists to perform in an all-stars band."

That was the all-stars band Nate said he was in every year.

Maybe this year, I'd be chosen. That would surprise Nate. And everyone else, too.

"There's also an exploring composers course," Mr. Byrd continued. "You can all Handel that, can't you?" He paused. "Get it? Handel? The composer?"

Sherman laughed. "Good one, sir!"

"And always remember, if it isn't baroque, don't fix it." Byrd was on a roll today.

"Huh?" Davis asked.

"Broke and baroque. That was a period of diverse music starting in the 1600s," Mr. Byrd said.

Davis nodded. "I'm digging it."

"And I'm digging your T-shirt," Mr. Byrd said.

Davis's parents are constantly buying him personalized T-shirts. This one said Band Beadle, with a cartoon beetle drumming on a rock.

I just shook my head. "When's free time?" I asked. Free time is my favorite camp activity.

"Immediately following supper, we have an evening rehearsal with all the other bands," Mr.

Byrd continued, reading from the schedule. "The rest of each night is free, with several organized events, like a dance, swimming relays, and various sports activities. At ten o'clock, it's lights out."

Finally, Mr. Byrd said, "Let's head to our cabins." Everybody followed him down a dirt path, lined on each side with pine trees.

Sherman came up beside me and whispered, "Zac, if anybody finds out you made a bet about winning Sound Off, you'll be in big trouble."

"Hey, it was Nate's idea. As long as you don't squeal, nobody'll ever know," I said.

But Sherman didn't seem so sure. He scooted closer to Lemuel Soriano. Lem plays trumpet. And he is, like, the perfect band student. He practices extra hard. He never forgets his sheet music or his instrument. And he never gets in trouble. Lem is pretty much the total opposite of me.

The trail ended and opened onto the middle of a giant field where we play games like kickball or

Wiffle ball in our free time. And where the kids who signed up for the marching class would practice. Back behind the field was a lake with a boat dock for fishing and kayaking.

On each side of the field were cabins. Boys on one side. Girls on the other. There were other buildings, too, like separate cabins for the band directors. High school band kids bunked with us in our cabins like camp counselors.

Then there was the band room where we'd practice every day. It was as big as our school gym. And the mess hall, where we'd eat. Plus, an outdoor amphitheater. That's where the Sound Off winner would be announced on the last day of camp.

"Mr. Byrd?" A teenaged girl came over. She wore a T-shirt with airbrushed butterflies fluttering above the name Janessa.

"Yes?" Mr. Byrd said.

"I'm assigned to a cabin with the Benton Bluff girls this week," Janessa said.

"Oh, good," Mr. Byrd said. "I remember you from last year, Janessa."

He should. Byrd goes to band camp every summer. He basically never takes a real vacation, which probably explains why he dresses like he's jetting off to some tropical island.

Janessa smiled and asked, "Are your campers ready to get settled in?"

"Absolutely! Girls, go with Janessa. Then we'll all meet back here beside these bleachers in, say," Mr. Byrd checked his watch, "half an hour."

I looked around for the teenager who'd bunk with us this week. Last year, we had this really cool kid named Preztin. He played sax, like me. And that dude seriously rocked.

But Byrd wasn't waiting. He headed toward the cabins, so we all followed behind him. I figured he'd veer off to a band director's cabin. He didn't. Instead, he marched straight toward our cabin.

"Here we are," he said. "Cabin six is ours."

Ours?

When Byrd opened the door and we went inside, I said, "You mean *ours*." I pointed to myself and then the other guys in the band. "Right?"

"No, I mean *ours*." Mr. Byrd pointed to all of us and then to himself. "There's a volunteer shortage this year, so they asked some of the band directors to bunk with their kids. No big deal."

Then Byrd plunked his suitcase on one of the cots.

I scrambled to find another cot. One far, far away from Byrd. I mean, he's my favorite teacher and all, but bunking that close to him would kill my fun. Seriously.

But by then, the other cots were already taken. "Great," I said, dropping my camouflage duffel bag onto my cot, right beside Byrd's.

After we were settled, Mr. Byrd said, "It's time to meet up with the girls. Move 'em out, boys." He held open the door, saying, "On the double!" as each one of us walked past.

The girls were already waiting for us when we got to the bleachers where we'd decided to meet.

"You'll never believe this," I whispered to Tally. "I'm stuck bunking beside Byrd."

"Why?" she asked.

"Not enough high schoolers. He volunteered."

"That's real dedication," Tally said.

"It's something, all right," I mumbled. "And you know what else is something?"

Tally shook her head.

I told her everything that had happened earlier with Nate and Ethan from Morrison Junior High. Well, almost everything. I left out the bet part.

"No way!" Tally said. "They seriously told you they'd beat us?"

"Yep. They said we'd go home crying."

"Not happening! We've gotta do something, Zac. They can't win."

See? I knew Tally would be all fired up about what Nate and Ethan had said. That's because besides band, Tally is a star on her snowboarding team and has won medals and everything. She doesn't like losing on the slopes. And she wouldn't like losing to the other bands at Sound Off, either.

"Tell me about it," I agreed. "But what?"

"Maybe start with telling Byrd."

"Nah. Do I look like a tattletale?"

"No," Tally said. "But Byrd should know. In case those kids try to start more trouble."

"They probably won't," I said. Plus, I didn't want Byrd to know about the part where they called him a goober. I mean, I didn't even tell Tally that. Just thinking about it sort of made me feel rotten. And more determined that our band would win.

Tally and I sat there for a few minutes. And then I finally said, "Hey, I got it! Let's take a look at the score sheet for Sound Off. Then we'll know how to score points with the judges."

"If we know how to get more points, we can focus on that and beat the other bands," Tally said.

"Exactly!" I grinned.

Tally high-fived me. "Zac, you're practically a genius."

"Please don't tell me you just figured that out," I joked.

Tally laughed.

Now we had a plan. But I was still afraid getting that clipboard away from Byrd wouldn't be easy.

Chapter 3

TALLY-ING POINTS

But the next morning in the mess hall, I got the chance I needed. The best part was I didn't even plan it. Sherman didn't know it, but he did all the work for me.

I'd just drizzled syrup on my pancakes when Tally plopped down across from me.

I blew the end of my straw wrapper at her. It hit her milk carton, bounced off, and nose-dived right in the middle of her pancakes. "Bull's-eye!"

"Zac!"

I laughed. "Hey, I was actually aiming at you, not your pancakes."

"Then your aim is terrible." Tally scraped the wrapper off her pancakes and flicked it at me.

"I'd talk," I said, dodging it.

Tally smiled. "So where is everybody?"

I looked around. Hardly anyone in our band had trays yet. "Looks like they're all still stuck in line behind Sherman," I said.

Even Byrd wasn't at a table yet. But his clipboard was. "Tally, look." I pointed.

She swallowed some milk. "Byrd's clipboard."

"This could be our chance," I said. "Let's swap tables."

We moved our trays to the table where Mr. Byrd would sit. That is, if he and everyone else ever got their food.

"What's taking Sherman so long, anyway?" I asked.

"I was right in front of him, and he was playing twenty questions with the cook. You know, stuff like—" She cleared her throat and pretended to be Sherman. "Are the pancakes gluten free? Is this organic orange juice? Could I get soy milk?"

I laughed. "Whoa! You sound just like him."

Sherman was big time into health and fitness. And right now, I was glad, because the breakfast line wasn't moving. At all.

"So I'll be your lookout." Tally glanced at Byrd.

I reached for his clipboard and flipped through the pages. "Not it. Not it. Hey, we're having pizza tomorrow," I said, scanning the menu.

"Zac, hurry!"

I kept flipping. "Not it. Not it. It! Here we go." Tally leaned across the table, trying to see. "What's it say? How do we earn points?"

"Hang on," I said. "I'm trying to read it, but so far blah, blah, all boring stuff." I skimmed to the bottom of the page. "Okay, here it is. Points are awarded for rhythm, tone quality, pitch, musicianship, preparation, technique, and performance."

I flipped over the page. "Plus, there are improvement points. And some points are given for sections and some for the entire ensemble."

"That's it?"

I held up one finger. "Nope. Bonus points for sight reading and song difficulty. And then there's something called the Wow Factor."

Tally frowned. "What's that?"

"It just says the judges are looking for something special, and they'll know it when they see it." I shook my head. "How are we supposed to know if we have the Wow Factor?"

"I get it," Tally said. "It's sort of like with snowboarding. Lots of people are good, but some snowboarders get people all pumped up. They wow the crowd."

"Like you?"

Tally grinned around the slice of bacon she nibbled on. "Maybe."

"So this'll be easier than I thought," I said. "All we gotta do is tell our band to wow the judges."

"Or else!" Tally added.

"Or else we lose," I said.

Tally glanced around again.

"Drop that clipboard! Here comes Sherman!" she said.

That meant the breakfast line was moving again. Byrd would get his food next.

"Greetings, fellow band campers!" Sherman's tray clinked against the metal table where Tally and I sat.

"Hey, Sherman," I said. "Thanks, dude!"

"For what?" Sherman eyed Byrd's clipboard suspiciously. "This feels like a crime scene. Is something illegal going on here?"

"Nah, no major crime," I said. Hey, that was true. It wasn't major. And sneaking a peek at Byrd's clipboard wasn't exactly a crime, either. Then I added, "I meant thanks for being you, Sherman. So Ethan and Nate better look out."

Sherman stuffed his mouth with eggs, but he looked confused.

"You'll find out when the Sound Off winner is announced," I explained. "But today, play your heart out on that flute. Really wow those judges, okay?"

Sherman stabbed a strawberry with his fork. He looked even more confused than before. "Uh, okay," he finally said.

"Great!" I said. "C'mon, Tally. We gotta get the rest of the band pumped up."

Tally and I put our trays away and then went table to table.

"Lem, how's that trumpet sound today?" I asked.

"Never better." Lem raised one eyebrow. "Why?"

"Because you've got to kill it for the judges." I jabbed the air. "Total knockout."

"Blow them away," Tally added.

"Got it?" I said.

"*Oui.* I'm the *crème de la crème.*" Lem jiggled his blue-framed glasses up and down. "That means the very best."

That was true. Lem is tops on trumpet, and he speaks French. Sort of. One time, we had this lame family tree assignment, and Lem found out he had some fancy French ancestor. Ever since, he's been using French words to impress us.

I gave Lem a thumbs-up before Tally and I headed to the next table where Kori Neal and Jack Cassilly sat.

"Hey, trombonists! Ready to wow the judges?"

Kori looked at me like I'd totally lost it, but she said, "Russell is always ready." Russell is what she named her trombone. "And so am I."

"Cool!" Tally high-fived Kori.

"What's the word, Third?" I asked Jack. I call him "Third" because his name is really Jack Cassilly III. "Are you pumped?"

"I don't mean to brag, but my trombone's the best at this camp," Jack said.

Of course, we all knew Jack meant to brag. His parents were super loaded. His instrument cost more than some people pay for a car. A nice one. Jack's trombone had to wow the judges.

I looked at Tally. "Wow Factor?"

She shrugged. "Maybe."

Next we headed over to Davis and Jasper Fava. They sat beating their drumsticks on their table, their trays, and even their juice cartons.

I saw the reflection of my head bobbing to the beat in the mirrored sunglasses Jasper always wears. "Dudes! You're gonna rock those judges," I said.

"Totally." Tally nodded. "You're awesome!"

"For sure!" Jasper smiled, not missing a beat.

Baylor must've overheard from the next table. "What's up, Zac?"

"Yeah, you gotta be pranking us," said Hope James, her best friend.

"Nah, no prank," I said.

"Why do you suddenly care so much about band?" Baylor asked. "I mean, it's a good thing, though. I like it." She twisted her long, black braid around one finger and smiled.

I smiled back. Then we just sort of stared at each other. With frozen smiley faces.

Then Sherman came over. "I know why!" he said.

My smile melted then. Sherman really did know more than I wanted everybody else to know. Before he blew it, I blurted out, "Simple. I think our band can win Sound Off."

"That's it?" Hope asked.

"Yep," I said.

"And the bet—" Sherman cut in.

"Beat. He means beat." I shot Sherman a "Shut it!" look. "Sherman's right. Truth is, I really want to beat all of those other bands."

"And that's why," Mr. Byrd said, coming over, "I don't want you focusing on points. Simply be your best." He looked down at his clipboard then. "Why is this thing sticky?"

Sherman looked like he was putting the clues together, so I said, "Sorry. I might've accidentally got some syrup on it, sir." And that was true, too. I didn't mean to get syrup on it when I was nosing through it earlier.

I grabbed Byrd's clipboard. "Lemme take care of it for you, sir." I slid it back and forth across my jeans, wiping the syrup away.

"Zac." Mr. Byrd reached for it.

"I've almost got it," I said.

"Zac!" He said again. "Hand it to me, please."

I did a few more swipes. But then, some of the pages came loose and the giant fans that cooled the mess hall blew them around everywhere.

"I got this," I said, chasing them down. And Baylor, Davis, and a couple of others helped, too.

When I finally handed them to Byrd, he took off his straw hat and fanned himself with it. "Thank you, Zac," he said real low.

"You're welcome, sir," I said.

Byrd smoothed the sheets on his clipboard and cleared his throat. "We're scheduled to play for the judges in twenty minutes. There should be a manila envelope with some sheet music that we've never seen before in our band mailbox. The mailbox is inside the office where we registered."

Byrd looked at me. "Zac, since you're full of energy this morning, would you get it for us, please?"

"Yes, sir. I'll be right back." And I ran as fast as I could to the office.

I'd show Byrd I wasn't a total goof-off. And when we played for the judges, our band would show 'em we had the Wow Factor. And when we got a ton of points, we'd really show Nate and Ethan we were the top band. Morrison was going down.

Chapter 4

MISSING MUSIC

When I got to the office at the end of the dirt path, I almost crashed right into Nate. Seriously, that kid was everywhere.

Aubrey was with him. She waved.

But Nate said, "Watch it, loser!" And as they walked away, he said over his shoulder, "I can't wait to see your new look in a few days."

Bet or no bet, he was *not* winning Sound Off.

"Hey, you'll be the one borrowing your band director's nail polish." But I didn't know if Nate heard me since they'd already disappeared through the trees lining the path.

I couldn't think about him right now, though. I had to grab our sheet music. Fast, too. Byrd and the rest of the band were waiting.

I took the steps to the office two at a time, and the screen door thwacked shut behind me as I ran inside. The band mailboxes were more like rows of mail slots all lined up in alphabetical order. But when I checked ours, it was empty. I even checked the other *B*'s in case there was some mix-up. The *A*'s and *C*'s, too. Nothing.

"Hey," I said to the teenager behind the desk. "Our band's envelope isn't here."

He was big time into some game on his phone.

"Have you seen it?" I tried again.

"Nope." He never even looked up.

Okay, he was zero help. But I couldn't go back and tell Byrd the envelope wasn't in our mailbox. Not yet, anyway. So I hung around outside on the front steps.

That's when a few kids from another band came along. I got sidetracked watching them toss instrument swabs up in the air. They made a game of seeing who could catch them. One came flying toward me, and I caught it. Then I wielded it like a sword.

"Nice," one kid said, using his like a sword, too.

And since I was still waiting to check our mailbox again, I got a great idea. "Hey, wanna have a sword fight?"

"Sure!" the kid said.

We played around, dueling each other with our instrument swab swords. And pretty soon, all of the other kids joined in, too. It was an epic battle. At least, it was until Kori and Lem showed up.

"Zac Wiles!" Kori shouted. "What're you doing?"

The kids I'd been hanging out with scrambled off then.

"*Oui*," Lem said. "Mr. Byrd sent us to see what's taking you so long. And you're goofing off."

"As usual," Kori added. "Where's our sheet music?"

"I dunno," I said.

"What do you mean?" Kori asked.

I held up my empty hands. "I mean, it wasn't in our mailbox."

Kori looked like she didn't believe me.

"Mr. Byrd won't be happy," Lem said. "But we have to go tell him."

He and Kori started back down the path.

When I didn't follow, Kori looked back. "Coming?"

I didn't want to. I knew Byrd would explode. *Kaboom!*

And when Kori and Lem told him I didn't have the envelope, he did. I'd never seen Byrd so mad.

"I sent you to get our sheet music, Zac. Instead, you clown around." He paced back and forth, flattening the grass beneath his flip-flops. "You squandered our preparation time before we meet with the judges. All of it."

"I know this looks bad, but I can explain," I finally said. This wasn't my fault. Not this time. "Our sheet music wasn't there."

Byrd stopped pacing. "What did you say?"

"When I checked our mailbox, it was empty," I said. "I was going to check again, but I sort of played around while I waited."

Byrd fanned himself with his hat. Again. "Let me get this straight. You're saying our sheet music never made it to our band mailbox?"

I nodded. "You got it."

"I want to believe you," Mr. Byrd said. "But in all my years here, there's never been such an error."

"Hey, it's a first," I said, shrugging my shoulders.

Mr. Byrd sighed. "Let's go speak with the judges. It's time for us to perform for them, anyway."

So we all followed Byrd into the band room.

"I'm sorry we're late," Mr. Byrd apologized to the judges. "It seems there may be a mix-up."

"What sort of mix-up?" one judge asked.

"Well, our sheet music wasn't in our mailbox this morning. I'm sorry to say we haven't had any preparation time before playing for you today."

Another judge frowned. "That's odd," she said. "I placed those envelopes in the mailboxes myself. I distinctly remember seeing a Benton Bluff Junior High envelope."

"I'm not sure what happened, ma'am," Mr. Byrd said. "Again, I apologize."

She nodded. "Give us a few moments, please."

While the judges whispered to each other, our band went over to the lockers that lined the wall. That's where we stored our instruments when we weren't using them. By the time we put our instruments together, the judges had reached a decision.

"I personally placed your envelope in your mailbox," the frowny-face judge began. "Since we can't conclude what happened after that, we're afraid you'll just have to play anyway. Here are your replacement copies."

Mr. Byrd took them. "You're asking us to play without any preparation?"

"Yes," she said. "Otherwise, every band could ask for special allowances. With our tight schedule, that's impossible."

"Whoa, hang on a sec. It's not our fault," I said.

Byrd made a slashing motion for me to stop.

"Be quiet, Zac," Kori whispered. "Are you trying to sink us on purpose?"

"No," I said. And hey, I wasn't trying to sink us at all. We had to win. Bragging rights between me and Nate and Ethan were riding on it. And so was our bet. Byrd looked just fine in his tropical shirts. But me wearing them? Nah. I'd much rather see Nate wearing his band director's skirt.

The judge frowned again. "We have to follow the rules. I'm sorry."

She didn't look that sorry to me, though. Not at all. But when the entire band glared at me, I got the feeling I was the one who'd really be sorry.

Byrd started passing out the sheet music.

"We've never even seen this before, Mr. Byrd," Sherman said, freaking out. "What are we supposed to do?"

"Your best," Mr. Byrd said. "Just play like the musicians you are. It'll be true sight-reading." Then he stood in front of the band with his arms up, signaling to us to have our instruments in place to begin. "One and two and ready and go . . ."

And we went all right. Straight down, sort of like skydiving without a parachute. Our timing was off. Our tone was all over the place. And our performance? It stunk. In other words, total disaster. The only good thing about it was when we got to the last measure. That's when the song finally ended and we could start pretending it never happened.

Byrd talked to the judges while we put away our instruments.

"So much for wowing the judges," Sherman said, latching his flute case.

"*Oui*," Lem said. "Was all that stuff at breakfast about killing our performance for the judges just another one of your jokes?"

"If it was, it wasn't very funny," Kori said.

I shrugged. "No, I was serious."

"That'd be a first," Hope said, squeezing past me.

Then Jack, Davis, and Jasper walked by in a huff, too. And even Baylor. She wasn't smiling at me now. At all.

I pulled my cap low over my eyes. "Man, with the looks y'all are shooting my way, I wish that camouflage really did make me invisible," I joked.

But nobody laughed. Even though it was a joke, I was sort of serious about wishing I were invisible.

I spent the rest of the day wishing that, too. Everybody was mad at me, except Tally. We'd both signed up for the marching band elective. When we finished for the afternoon, she came over and we walked off the field together.

"Left, left, left, right, left," Tally said, matching her steps to mine all the way over to the bleachers. "Is it weird that even after practice, I can't stop walking in step with someone?"

"Nah, it's weirder that you're still talking to me. Everybody else wants to zap me right outta band." I kicked at an empty water bottle lying on the grass.

"Not me." Tally stooped to pick up the bottle. "When I first joined band, it was like I had to choose between the snowboarders and the band geeks. Remember?"

"Yep, everybody was mad at you."

"And you and Jasper were basically the only ones who talked to me. The band got over it." She tossed me the bottle. "They'll get over this, too."

"Maybe. But you know what's really funny?" I asked.

Tally shook her head.

"I wouldn't have cared before. But now I do. I mean, I didn't even wanna be in band at first. My parents signed me up."

"Same way my grandparents signed me up," Tally said. "They said I needed to learn a life skill. You know, something besides snowboarding."

"No wonder. Some of your tricks wouldn't be so hot at ninety. Your false teeth would fly right outta your mouth. *Smack!* They'd land on the judge's table," I joked.

"Exactly!" Tally laughed. Then she asked, "Did your parents sign you up so you'd do something besides fishing?"

Hanging out at the lake with my rod and reel is my favorite thing in the world. Everybody knows it. But that isn't why I'm in band. The real reason is hard to talk about. And I don't tell a lot of people. I crunched the water bottle in my hand, watching the plastic get smaller.

"Sometimes," I finally began, "I can't focus on stuff. My mind sort of races, and I can't make it stop." I shrugged. "Like, it took me forever to learn to read."

Tally didn't say anything.

"Anyway, my parents hoped band would help me focus. And at first, I hated it," I admitted.

She smiled. "Me too. But now I love band. And the band geeks."

"So do I." And that wasn't something I told a lot of people either. "But don't tell anybody. Or else."

"Or else what?" Tally grinned.

I held up the flattened water bottle and smiled. "Your French horn will look just like this."

"Uh-oh." Tally laughed and pretended to zip her lips.

I laughed, too, and tossed the bottle into the recycling bin beside the bleachers.

By then, the rest of the band and Byrd were gathering there, too.

Byrd tucked his clipboard in his armpit and clapped his hands to get everyone's attention. "Okay, gang. Next on our schedule is full band rehearsal. That means we'll practice with all of the camp bands."

"We can't face those judges," Lem said. "Not after what happened this morning."

"Thanks to Zac," Kori added.

"Hey, I'm sorry. But it really wasn't my fault," I said.

Byrd made waving motions with his hands. "That's water under the bridge now. Let's dry ourselves off and move on." Then he pointed to the band room. "Forward. March!"

Everyone filed in behind him all the way to the band room. With all of the bands in there at one time, the place was packed. And loud. And crazy.

But our band really did move on at full band rehearsal, just like Byrd said. One judge said our pitch was accurate and our beat was right on. Even the frowny-face judge from this morning said we were the most improved band of the day. I knew from peeking at Byrd's Sound Off score sheet that we'd get some major points for that.

When rehearsal ended, things got even crazier. Everyone was shoving, trying to get to their lockers. Unlucky for me, Nate's locker was near mine. He and Ethan hung around while I opened my locker. Aubrey was there, too.

"Do you think you'll make the all-stars band again this year?" Ethan asked.

"Sure," Nate said. "I always do."

So I said, "Don't count on it. The judges at the sax workshop said I have a shot at it."

Nate pretended he just noticed me then. And he grinned so big I didn't see how his face fit inside the band room. "Hey, Wiles. I heard your band lost some sheet music this morning. That'll really drop your Sound Off points, huh?"

"Yeah." Ethan smiled, too. "You're so gonna win this bet, Nate."

Nate leaned back against the locker and propped his hands behind his head. "No worries."

"Don't be so sure." I stuffed my sax case inside my locker and slammed the door shut.

"I wonder," Nate gazed up at the fluorescent lights overhead, like he was thinking hard, "what could've happened to that sheet music?"

Ethan stared at the lights, too. "Yeah, I wonder."

Then they both died laughing and ran out of the band room.

And I wondered something, too. Did Nate really know what had happened to our sheet music?

Chapter 5

SPAGHETTI FINGERS

The next day, Byrd didn't send me to our band mailbox. He sent Baylor instead. The entire band hung around outside the band room waiting for her.

Most of us boys took turns seeing who could jump over the bushes that grew beneath the windows.

"Hey, dudes! Check it out." Jasper pointed to a small door near the ground.

"What's that, Mr. Byrd?" Sherman asked.

"Just an old storm cellar," he explained.

Just then, Baylor came back, waving the manila envelope with our sheet music inside like it was a victory flag.

"Baylor's a hero!" I cheered.

She really was. Now we wouldn't lose points like we did yesterday. And maybe I wouldn't lose the Sound Off bet with Nate.

But Baylor frowned. She was still mad at me about yesterday. And so was everybody else.

Then Hope clapped. Baylor blew victory kisses into the air when other kids clapped, too.

The clapping didn't end outside of the band room, though. Since we actually had time to review our music, we rocked our song. Even the judges clapped after we played for them. They had tons of positive comments for us, too.

When the frowny-face judge said we had a particularly strong woodwind section, Sherman, Baylor, and Hope high-fived me.

"See? I told you." Tally elbowed me.

She was right. The band was already forgetting to be mad at me. For the rest of the day, things only got better. Until that afternoon when it was time for full band rehearsal again.

One judge stood at the front of the band room and tapped his watch. "We will start promptly in five minutes," he said.

"That means get your instruments and get in your seats," Mr. Byrd's voice boomed above the crowd. So we all scrambled to our lockers to grab our instruments.

I swung my locker door open and reached inside. But instead of grabbing my saxophone case, I got a handful of today's leftover lunch. Cold, jiggly spaghetti noodles.

Sherman laughed his guts out and called me Spaghetti Fingers when he saw me trying to scrape off the noodles.

"Good one, Sherman," I said, but I laughed, too. I had to give it to him, it was a funny prank, especially for a kid who basically never joked around. Not when it came to band, anyway. "You know, hiding someone's instrument is classic," I said. "But replacing it with pasta, now that's a twist."

"Yeah," Sherman said, catching his breath from laughing so hard. "It really is." Then he grabbed his flute case from his locker and took off.

"Wait!" I called after him.

Sherman stopped and turned around. "Yeah?"

"Dude! Where's my saxophone?"

"I dunno." Sherman shrugged. "Check the mess hall. It's probably underneath a pile of meatballs."

"I get it. Spaghetti and meatballs." I smiled. But by now, most kids were already in their seats. This was going too far. "Seriously, Sherman! Where's my sax, dude?"

"Beats me." Then Sherman struck a yoga pose in front of his stand before joining the other flutes.

Okay, he wasn't kidding. Sherman didn't have my sax. This seriously wasn't funny. Not anymore.

I had two choices. I could tell Byrd my sax was missing. Then he and the whole band would think I was goofing off and get mad all over again when they'd just gotten un-mad at me. Or I could find my sax myself. Fast!

It was a no-brainer. Before rehearsal started, I rummaged through some of the lockers beside mine. Empty. All of them. It reminded me of yesterday with our empty band mailbox. And I got a bad feeling.

"Let's begin by running through some scales," one of the judges said. "Afterward, we'll play the 'Squishy, Wishy Watermelon' song."

But there wouldn't be any scales or squishy watermelons for me. Not without my sax. I had to find it. The band couldn't lose any more points because of me. And I couldn't lose my bet.

If I were a saxophone, where would I hide? I squatted low behind the percussion section and sort of crawled around the back of the room, searching everywhere. Aha! I spotted something black between Davis and Jasper's snare drums.

But when I grabbed for it, I bumped into Davis and he got off beat. "Get up, Zac. You're messing me up," he whispered.

"For real, man," Jasper said. "You can clown around later. After rehearsal."

Turned out, it was a case between their drums. Just not mine.

"Sorry," I said. "But I can't find my sax."

"Why don't you check the woodwind section, dude?" Jasper suggested, never missing a beat.

"Good idea," I said. "Thanks!"

So I scooted army style down the aisle, slowly sneaking past the tubas and the French horns. But I got a little too close to the trombones. Kori almost emptied her spit valve on me.

I finally made it to the woodwinds, and I squeezed under Baylor's chair. See? Every time I'd embarrassed my mom crawling under people's chairs when I was little was about to pay off.

Baylor's clarinet squeaked when she noticed me, but she kept on playing. I kept right on inching along. Slowly, like a worm. That was the trick.

Next, I wedged myself under Yulia Glatt's chair. And Lilly's. Then the chair of some girl wearing a fuzzy toe ring. Or maybe she'd braided the hair on her toe. I wasn't sure. I almost found out, though, when she kicked off her flip-flops. Her big toe barely missed my mouth. *That was a close one.*

Then I was almost to Sherman's chair. I recognized his gray sneakers. But first, I had to crawl past some guy with sweaty feet that smelled like moldy cheese. *Ew!* I could've died under his chair. No joke!

I grabbed the legs of Sherman's chair to get more leverage. When I did, he must've felt it because he stopped playing his flute and looked down.

I waved. But Sherman didn't wave back. Instead, he opened his mouth. I put my fingers up to my lips to shush him. Too late. He let out a scream that sounded worse than a band room filled with geeks on their first day of practice.

Everyone froze mid-song, and the room went silent. Deadly silent.

Until high heels clicked across the floor, headed my way. Then the frowny-face judge knelt down and took a peek at me lying on the floor under Sherman's chair.

I waved and gave her my best sheepish smile.

But she was just like Sherman. She didn't wave back, either. The frown line between her eyebrows got deep enough to hide a tube of cork grease when she said, "I demand that you come out from underneath that chair. This instant!"

"Yes, ma'am." I crawled out and dusted off my clothes.

"Come with me, young man."

I followed her up front to a table where the band directors sat. Byrd was already on his feet when she asked him, "Isn't this your student?"

Byrd looked from her to me. At first, I wasn't even sure he'd admit to being my teacher. But he finally nodded. "Yes, indeed. He is one of mine."

"Very well." She folded her arms across her chest. "Please deal with this issue."

"I was looking for my saxophone," I tried to explain. "Somebody took it from my locker."

"Just like somebody took our sheet music?" Mr. Byrd's eyebrows shot up above his glasses.

"Exactly," I said. "Whoever took our music probably took my sax, too."

"That's enough, Zac," Mr. Byrd said. Then he told all of the judges, "I apologize for Zac's behavior, and I assure you this problem will be resolved immediately."

"See that it is," the frowny-face judge said.

"Zac," Mr. Byrd said, "let's step outside. Now."

Before we headed out into the sunlight, I took one last look at the other kids. You know, in case Byrd banished me from band forever and I never saw them again. Not in the band room, anyway.

Tally looked surprised. Sherman looked confused. And then there was Nate. He smiled so big he could probably stuff the mouthpieces of every saxophone in the room in his mouth. Maybe the clarinets, too.

Nate was totally up to something. I wasn't sure what yet, but I'd find out. Nate could bet on it.

Chapter 6

SAX-STEALING ALIENS

"Zac, please don't get us kicked out of camp," Mr. Byrd said when we stood outside the band room.

"Hey, someone seriously took our music," I said. "And my sax. I promise."

"And someone forced you, completely against your will, to crawl beneath everyone's chairs. Yes?"

When Byrd said it like that, it sounded totally crazy. "Not exactly . . . ," I began.

He held up one hand. "I'm sorry, but this lines up with your past irresponsible behavior."

"I know. But this time, I really did put my sax case in my locker. And it just disappeared! *Poof!*"

"Work some magic and make it reappear. Okay?" Mr. Byrd sighed. "One person can't make a band. But one person can break it. Please remember we're counting on you, Zac."

I nodded. "Yes, sir."

"I'm going back inside for rehearsal. Look hard. I'm sure you'll find your saxophone." And with that, he was gone.

Byrd said to make my sax reappear. I'd already tried that. But I was no magician. I was pretty sure I knew who'd made it *disappear*, though. Nate.

"Aliens," Sherman said.

"Huh?" I asked.

"Tell him, Davis," Sherman said.

It was evening free time. I'd been searching and searching for my saxophone. Davis had even helped me look. So had Sherman since he felt bad for being the one to scream and get me busted for crawling under the chairs. But hey, I probably would've freaked out, too. Anyway, still no sax.

They did have some theories on what happened, though. Davis was big time into doodling cartoons, so he'd even sketched his hypothesis. So while we took turns seeing who could toss his drumsticks the farthest, Davis whipped out his drawing pad.

"Check this out," he said, flipping through the pages. "Aliens swooped into camp and morphed into band directors. Then they beamed your sax up to their planet."

"What if the judges really are aliens?" Sherman asked. "This could be part of their cosmic plan."

"It's possible," Davis said.

"Dudes! You've both lost it."

Okay, maybe not completely. The frowny-face judge had all these neck wrinkles. A sure sign of an alien. You know, for quick face mask switcheroos.

"Or," Sherman went on, "what if there's a secret passageway in the back of Zac's locker?"

"Creepy." Davis slapped his drawing pad shut. "Let's go check it out."

"If we're not back in an hour, come check your locker, Zac," Sherman called over his shoulder.

"I will," I promised.

Tally came over then. "You will what?"

"You know, free Sherman and Davis from the secret portal in my locker. Unless the alien judges beam them up first."

She laughed. "You guys are nuts."

"Probably," I agreed. "Wanna watch the kickball game?" I pointed at the bleachers.

We sat, and Tally asked, "Still no sax?"

"Nope. Don't be surprised when there's a movie made about me. *Zac Wiles: The Only Kid in History Who Never Returned from Band Camp.*"

I mean, I couldn't go home. My parents are used to me misplacing my neck strap or my mouthpiece. Hey, that's usually on purpose. But this was my entire saxophone. A way bigger deal.

"That's a super long movie title." Tally laughed again.

Then she got serious. "What do you think really happened to your sax, Zac?"

My theory didn't involve aliens and portals. It involved rats. A human rat, to be exact. I leaned closer to Tally and whispered one word, "Nate."

"For real? You think he, like, sabotaged you?"

"Hey, I don't want to accuse him without proof, or anything," I said. "But when Byrd kicked me out, you should've seen Nate's face. He loved it."

Tally nodded. "That reminds me of when this snowboarder kept finding her gear damaged in the locker room. A bunch of us started following the girl we thought was doing it. We caught her in the act and she landed in big trouble."

"Good. She should've."

"Totally," Tally said.

Maybe I could start following Nate. Then I'd know for sure. But that seemed sort of weird.

"I'm just gonna ask Nate if he took my sax," I finally said.

Tally shielded her eyes from the setting sun. "Here's your chance. Isn't that him heading our way now?"

Ethan was with him, of course. They plopped down on the bleachers in front of us and talked loud enough for us to hear on purpose.

Nate said, "Man, we're skunking those other bands."

"Are you surprised?" Ethan asked.

Nate shook his head. "No way! We're the best."

"We've got a ton of Sound Off points already," Ethan went on.

"Psh! We're way up here." Nate held one hand way up high. "And everyone else is way down here." He held his other hand way down low.

Ethan laughed.

Nate wasn't finished yet, though. "That one band is the worst." He looked at Ethan.

"Which one?"

Nate grinned. "Barfin' Bluff!"

Ethan slapped Nate's shoulder like it was the funniest thing he'd ever heard.

I'd had enough. "Dudes! You're *hilarious*," I said sarcastically. "And hey, it's easy to have the most points when you hide stuff from other campers."

Nate's smile faded then. "Wiles, are you saying I took your band's sheet music? And your sax?"

"Yeah," I said. "That's exactly what I'm saying. 'Cause you seemed pretty happy when my sax was missing today."

Nate shrugged. "So what? Just because I laughed doesn't mean I did it."

"You're just jealous because Nate will make the all-stars band again and you don't have a shot," Ethan said. "Anyway, Nate wouldn't steal your sax."

"Thanks, man" Nate said. "Here's an idea. Maybe your girlfriend can find your sax for you, Zac-y-poo."

"Whoa, she's not my—" I began.

And Tally said, "Girlfriend."

"How sweet," Ethan said. "She finishes his sentences."

"Awww," Nate cooed. Then he noticed Aubrey walk past. "Let's leave these lovebirds alone. Later, losers!" He and Ethan barreled down the bleachers to catch up with Aubrey.

So that was sort of awkward. Everyone knows Tally and Jasper like each other.

Luckily, Sherman and Davis came back then, which helped us ignore any weirdness.

"Hey, you didn't find any secret passageways, did you? Or any sax-stealing aliens?" I joked.

"Nope, no aliens," Sherman said. "Just Aubrey."

"And she talked to Sherman." Davis made a kissy face.

"Nah, Aubrey's got a thing for Nate," I said. That was easy to see.

"Oh, and those dudes you were just talking to were in there, too," Davis said.

"Nate and Ethan?" I asked.

"Yep," Sherman said. "But when we walked in, they left."

Tally and I looked at each other.

"We have to follow Nate," she said.

That sort of creeped me out a little. Tally wasn't my girlfriend, like Nate said, but she was a really good friend. And she'd just read my mind. Because following Nate was exactly what I was thinking about. We'd start tonight, at the dance.

Chapter 7
DANCE TO THE BEAT

"Hey, check out the surfing geckos!"

I said back at our cabin before the dance. Byrd's tropical shirt lay neatly folded on his cot beside mine. The price tag still dangled from the collar. "Twenty-five bucks."

"I'd pay Byrd twenty-five bucks to return it," Jack said.

I laughed. Then I got an idea. "I dare you to try it on, Jack."

"Forget it, dude," Jack carefully patted his blond head. "I just gelled my hair."

I rolled my eyes. Jack fussed over his hair more than anyone I knew. "How about you, Davis?"

"Nuh-uh. I'm not wearing Byrd's shirt." Davis shook his head.

"Why don't you try it on, Zac?" Sherman said. "It was your idea."

"Yeah!" Jack and Davis agreed.

"Fine. I will." Slipping it over my head was sort of like a dress rehearsal, just in case I lost the bet I'd made with Nate. Not that I planned on losing.

"It's way too big for you," Sherman said. "It looks more like my grandma's jumbo-sized muumuus."

Now I had an audience. Jasper and Lem had gathered around, too. So I stood up straight, clapped my hands, and said in my sternest Mr. Byrd voice, "Enough of this clowning around, boys." I raised my arms in front of me. "One and two and ready and play."

At first, they all looked at me like the sun had melted my brain today. But when Sherman held his pretend flute up to his lips and pressed some fake keys, everybody else joined in, too.

Jack moved the slide on his imaginary trombone. Lem blew into his air trumpet. Jasper and Davis beat their make-believe drumsticks. And I directed them, wildly waving my arms around, with Byrd's floppy shirtsleeves flapping along.

The band sounded amazing. You know, in my head. But suddenly, they stopped playing. *Poof!* All of their air instruments disappeared.

"Don't quit now. Play like the musicians you are!" I encouraged them with one of Byrd's favorite band room lines.

But nobody even cracked a smile. Sherman shook his head. Then Jasper pointed behind me.

I spun around. Slowly.

It was Byrd. Of course it was Byrd. He leaned against the screen door, watching the show.

"Er, hello, sir," I began. "I'll just take this off now." I fumbled over his shirt's buttons.

"Stop!" Mr. Byrd raised one hand, and I froze.

"There's a big problem here," he said, making his way toward us. "Does anyone know what that problem is?"

"Zac?" Sherman guessed.

Thanks a lot, Sherman.

"No, Zac isn't the problem," Mr. Byrd finally said. "The problem is, this band needs a guitarist." He pretended to strum a chord. "Rock and roll, dudes!"

We all died laughing. Even Byrd was having fun at camp, and everyone jammed along with him. We rocked until Byrd said it was time to head to the dance.

When I handed Byrd his gecko shirt back, he smiled and said, "It looked great on you, Zac."

"Thanks," I said. "But I'll stick with camouflage."

"Not tonight," Mr. Byrd said. "Please wear something a little more dance appropriate."

So I tugged on a black button-down shirt my mom had insisted I pack. Then I headed to the outdoor amphitheater where the dance was being held. And where Tally and I planned to meet up to spy on Nate and Ethan.

Paper lanterns bobbed in the nighttime breeze. Strings of lights overhead cast a glow over the crowd. And over the buffet table, piled high with snacks.

All of the different bands would take turns playing songs while the other campers danced. Our band was scheduled to play later on. Of course, I wouldn't be playing. Not unless my sax showed up. Soon.

"There they are, Tally!" I pointed to the stage.

Nate and Ethan were already up there with their band. Nate's sax was attached to his neck strap. And he was talking to Aubrey. He teased me about having a girlfriend. But look at him. He and Aubrey were always together.

"We're from Morrison Junior High," their band director, Mrs. Hendrix, said into the microphone then. "Tonight, we're starting off with a fast song, so get up on your feet!" She motioned for everyone to stand up before turning to face her band.

As soon as the music started, people began dancing. And since Nate wasn't leaving the stage anytime soon, I figured we may as well dance, too.

"C'mon, Tally! Let's go!" I shouted above the band.

We squeezed onto the dance floor with all of the other kids. Davis sort of karate kicked the air to the beat. Sherman did this leaping frog hop move. Up and down. The curls in his hair almost bounced right into the stars above us. And Jasper's mirrored sunglasses reflected it all.

It was so much fun I almost forgot about my missing sax. Almost.

Then the song ended, and Lem and Kori headed my way.

"Zac, how can you dance when your sax is still missing?" Kori asked. "Shouldn't you be looking for it?"

"*Oui*," Lem said. "You're costing us points with the judges, *monsieur*."

"Hey, what'd you just call me, Lem?"

"*Monsieur*," he said again. "It means mister."

I should've thanked Nate then, I guessed. His band started playing another song, so I didn't have to listen to Kori and Lem anymore. For now.

But this song wasn't fast. It was one of those slow songs that couples sway back and forth to.

Lem and Kori danced together. Then I noticed Jasper coming our way.

"Wanna dance?" he asked.

"Dude, I'd love to," I joked.

Jasper adjusted the American flag bandana he wore on his forehead. "Not you, man." He smiled and held out his hand. "Tally?"

Tally's cheeks turned pink as she took his hand, and they began to sway, too.

Okay, so when you're not half of a couple, slow dances are totally painful. I decided to join

Sherman and Davis at the buffet table. But on my way, I bumped into Baylor.

"Would you like to dance?" She wound one braid around her finger.

"Maybe. Let me ask my agent." That whole agent thing was sort of an inside joke. It started one time when Baylor roped me into planning a band pizza party. So I pretended to think about it and grinned. "Sure."

We swayed along with everyone else. Usually at the school dances in our gym, the girls hang out on one side and the boys on the other. So I hadn't danced with very many girls in my life. I wasn't sure if we were supposed to silently sway, or if talking while swaying was allowed.

But I finally said, "Nice brows. I mean, bards. I mean, those bows tied on your braids look nice." *Super smooth, Zac,* I told myself. Sometimes when Baylor and I are together, my tongue acts really dumb. Jumbled up words come spilling out.

"Thanks." Baylor smiled. Then she cleared her throat. "You know, I have this reporter's sixth sense about people. So I can sniff things out."

I wrinkled my nose and fanned the air. "Don't tell anybody, but that smell? It's Sherman. He left his deodorant at home," I joked.

"Zac!" Baylor poked my ribs. "I'm serious. And I'm talking about your saxophone."

I made a straight face then. "Sorry. What's your sixth sense telling you? If it can find my sax, I'll owe you big time."

"Remember when you helped me make decorations for the band party a few months ago?"

"Yep. You were jealous because my treble clefs were way more glittery than yours," I teased.

Baylor rolled her eyes. "So was my carpet."

"Hey, I'm still sorry about glitter bombing your house."

"It's gone now. Mostly. Anyway," Baylor said, "you told me when you first learned to read, the letters got all mixed up. And that sometimes it happens with music notes, too."

I didn't say anything.

"It's okay, Zac," Baylor went on. "I know it must be hard. But you don't have to hide the band's sheet music and your saxophone to get out of playing."

"What?" Was she serious? I mean, my letters did used to get flip-flopped. And sometimes my brain feels like it's doing a sprint inside my head. When it races, the music notes flip-flop, too. But I didn't hide my sax because of it.

Somebody else did. And I had a feeling I knew who that somebody was. Nate. All I needed was evidence. But I was facing away from the stage and couldn't keep an eye on him. So I figured out how to slowly sway and turn. Sway. Then turn. And after a few swaying turns, Nate was back on my radar.

The music stopped then. And I spotted Nate practically running off the stage. Ethan, too.

"Hey, I gotta go," I said.

Baylor grabbed my shoulder. "Wait, I'm sorry if I made you mad."

"Nah, it's not like that. I'm not mad." I smiled to prove it. "But stay tuned, Miss Reporter. There's going to be a breaking story soon."

I took off after Nate.

But Byrd stopped me. He looked way better in his surfing geckos shirt than I did earlier. "Zac, I know you don't have your instrument, but I would like for you to sit onstage with the rest of the band. Please join us for warm-ups."

"When?" I asked.

"Now," Mr. Byrd said.

Stop the presses. Tonight's breaking story just got canned. Maybe there'd be big news to report tomorrow. I still had hope.

Chapter 8
CAUGHT YA!

"Last night was a total bust," I said to Tally after breakfast the next morning.

"Definitely," she agreed. "And tomorrow's the last day of camp already."

"Believe me, I know." I'd been practicing how to break it to my parents that I'd lost my saxophone. So far, I only had my opening line. Something like, "You'll never believe this!" I didn't worry about coming up with anything else after that. Because by then, I'd already be like Sherman's gluten-free bread this morning. Toast.

Two days. That's all we had to find out what Nate did with my saxophone. So when he and Ethan scooted their chairs back and left the mess hall in a rush, we got our chance.

Tally and I followed them all the way to the camp office. Nate and Ethan went inside. We hid behind a tree on the other side of the path and watched them through the window. Sort of.

Tally peeked around the tree trunk. "What's going on?"

"I dunno." I shrugged. "I can't see."

"Here comes somebody," Tally whispered.

"Get down," I said. "They'll spot your red shirt."

We both sank lower into the weeds growing around the gnarled tree roots.

"See?" I said. "This is why I always wear camouflage."

Tally nodded. "Yeah. Because you never know when you're gonna need to hide behind trees to spy through the windows at band camp. Right?"

She was totally being sarcastic, but I didn't mind. Because what Tally said was true. Blending with your surroundings could be important sometimes. Like now.

When the footsteps sounded closer on the path, I peeked above the weeds. "Hey, it's Aubrey," I said.

She went inside the office, too.

"I wonder what they're up to," Tally said.

I stood up. "There's only one way to find out."

"Zac!" Tally grabbed my arm. "Are you crazy? We can't just go in there."

"Why not?" I asked. "Nate's probably stealing our sheet music again. Right now."

Tally leaned against the tree trunk, not budging.

"Hey, you can go in or wait out here. Your choice," I said, heading toward the office.

"Wait!" Tally scrambled after me. "I'm in. But what's our plan?"

"Simple. We storm the office and catch Nate stealing our music."

"Gotcha."

So we sneaked up the steps. I grabbed the doorknob with one hand and silently mouthed, *One, two, three.* Then I tugged open the door.

Then I yelled, "Caught ya!"

But Nate wasn't even near the band mailboxes. Neither was Ethan.

"Caught us doing what, loser?" Nate asked, holding a broom and a dustpan. "Sweeping?"

"Emptying trash?" Ethan held up a black bag.

"You mean, you work in the office?" Tally asked.

"Every morning. The camp always needs volunteers, you know," Aubrey added.

Then Nate emptied the dustpan into Ethan's trash bag. Ethan tied it up and set it by the door.

"Sorry, dude. About yelling just then," I said.

Nate nodded. "Look, I know you think I'm stealing stuff. But it's like I told you. I didn't do it. And I don't like being accused of stuff I didn't do."

"Yeah, man. Just lay off Nate, would you?" Ethan said.

"Stop following me around. Then maybe you'll find out who really did it," Nate suggested. "I gotta go. I volunteered to sweep the band room, too."

All three of them took off, taking the trash with them. I watched through the screen door as they shoved it into the dumpster.

"Wow," Tally finally said. "I really thought Nate was doing this stuff. Guess I was way off."

I didn't say anything.

"Zac, you don't still think it was Nate. Do you?"

"I just have this bad feeling about him."

"So now what?" Tally asked.

"No idea. But since we're here, let's grab today's music from our mailbox to surprise everyone."

"Okay. You get it, and I'll wait outside. There was a squirrel in the big maple tree when we walked in," Tally said, pulling her phone from her pocket.

"So you're gonna call him?" I joked.

"No, I'm gonna snap his picture. He was cute."

"Cuter than Jasper?" I drew an air heart.

"Cut it out!" Tally smiled, heading outside.

While I was still in the office, the phone rang. "This is Zac," I said into the receiver.

It was some band director asking to speak to the camp nurse. She said something about poison ivy affecting her musicians.

"Sorry. She's not here right now," I said.

After she hung up, I grabbed our sheet music envelope. Then some other campers came in. They hurried over to their mailbox, too.

"Wait! Our envelope isn't here," one boy said.

The girl that was with him looked at my hand. "How come yours is but ours isn't?" she asked.

"I dunno," I said.

Then the same girl said, "Isn't that the guy from Benton Bluff who lost their music?"

"I think so," the boy said.

"Maybe we should tell on him," the girl said.

"I'm standing right here. I can hear you talking about me, you know," I said.

But they both ignored me.

"Why would he take ours?" the boy asked.

"Think about it. To knock us out of some points," the girl went on.

Now I sort of knew how Nate felt. I didn't like being accused of something I didn't do either. Maybe I was wrong about him after all.

"Nah, it's too bad about your envelope," I said. "But I didn't take it. I promise."

Tally was at the door then. "Zac, are you coming? We're going to be late."

"Yeah, I'm coming," I said.

I followed Tally out the door without saying anything else to the other campers.

We headed to the band room and everyone had probably our best practice yet. Well, except me. Since I still didn't have my sax, Byrd made me sit beside him while he directed. To keep me out of trouble, he said.

The band played a song called "Loop-de-loop Fair." Even the frowny-face judge was impressed.

"Your tone is consistent and clear," she said. "And your dynamics are impeccable."

If she wasn't careful, her frown might just cartwheel into a smile.

But it didn't last. After full band rehearsal that evening, the frowny-face judge frowned more than ever when she said, "Mr. Byrd, I'd like to speak with you. And your student."

"Zac, what have you done now?" Mr. Byrd said under his breath.

"Nothing, sir," I said.

But what the frowny-face judge said next wasn't nothing. It was huge.

Chapter 9

SO BUSTED

Mr. Byrd sent everyone else in the band outside while he and I met with the judges.

"I'm sorry to inform you," the frowny-face judge began, "that there have been allegations brought against this young man here."

"Al-uh-what-y?" I asked.

"It means someone has accused you of something, Zac," Mr. Byrd explained.

The frowny-face judge nodded. "Several people have come forward, in fact. It seems as the day has progressed, numerous items have disappeared. It began this morning when other bands were missing sheet music from their mailboxes."

I knew that girl in the office this morning would rat on me. It was her scary, tattletale eyes.

"We interviewed several band directors. And Mrs. Hendrix, Morrison's director, mentioned she'd also called the office this morning to speak with the nurse about a case of poison ivy," the frowny-face judge continued. "And guess who answered the phone?"

"Zac?" Mr. Byrd said.

"Indeed." She nodded.

"Yeah, but Tally was with me," I said. "She knows I didn't take any other band's sheet music."

"That could shed new light on things," a different judge said. "Was she with you the entire time?"

"No," I admitted. "She went to snap a picture of a squirrel when the phone rang. And while I got our envelope." I looked at Byrd then. "I only wanted to surprise you with our sheet music this morning."

"This is a surprise, all right." Mr. Byrd folded his arms. Then he asked the judges, "Is that all?"

Another judge chimed in. "I'm afraid not. Other bands have now reported missing instruments."

"See?" I said. "I told you I wasn't goofing off. Somebody really did take my sax." And I couldn't wait until they caught that somebody. Named Nate.

The frowny-face judge took a deep breath. "I'm glad you brought that up. It's been suggested that perhaps you took your own instrument. And now you're taking other instruments as well."

"What? That's crazy!" I said. "Why would I do that?"

"Why, indeed. We've wondered that, too." The frowny-face judge leaned back in her seat. "Possibly to cover up the fact that you took your own instrument in the first place. Also, to ensure the other bands dropped in their Sound Off point standings."

"No way!" I looked at Byrd. "You gotta believe me. I didn't take any sheet music or instruments. Not mine. And not anybody else's, either."

"Calm down, Zac. I'm sure we'll find a reasonable explanation for all of this."

Yeah, I was sure we would, too. If we could get Nate to do some explaining, that is. But I didn't even waste my oxygen saying that. Nobody'd believe me, anyway.

When we got free time that night, everybody in the whole camp heard the rumor that I'd taken the other campers' instruments. I got tired of everybody staring at me and whispering stuff, so I hung out by the lake at the edge of the field. Jasper, Baylor, Sherman, Davis, and Tally had stuck around for a while. But then they all took off to play Wiffle ball and I stayed behind.

Hitting a ball with a bat might've made me feel better. But I didn't really want to hang out with a lot of people right now. I sat on the boat dock by myself, watching dragonflies skim over the water in the moonlight.

"They're pretty cool, aren't they?" Tally said.

"Hey, you're back," I said. "Is the game over?"

"Nope. But you looked lonely down here by yourself." Tally smiled. "And we have work to do."

I wasn't sure what she meant. "Work?"

"Yep. We've got instruments to find."

"Give it up, Detective Tally," I said.

She sort of laughed.

"Hey, that's a pity laugh. You're just trying to make me feel better."

Tally knew I was in big-time trouble. Byrd had no choice. He'd called my parents to fill them in on what had happened. If the instruments weren't found, they might even have to pay for them.

But worst of all, I'd probably get kicked out of band. Maybe band didn't come easy for me. I had to work harder than other kids to focus. But when I finally got a song, the extra work felt worth it. Kinda lame. But true.

And I was going to miss hanging out with everybody in band. Even Byrd. No joke.

"There's only one thing that'll make you feel better," Tally said. "And that's busting Nate." She grabbed my arm. "C'mon."

"Where are we going?"

"To the band room. Nate took your sax, so maybe you should take his hostage."

"Have you totally lost it?" I asked.

"Nope," Tally said. "But hopefully Nate will when his sax is gone. Then he'll spill his guts and give yours back."

Tally's idea was terrible. But it was my last chance to prove I didn't take those other instruments. I didn't have a choice.

"Let's go," I said.

As we sneaked toward the band room, I whispered, "Shh. Walk quietly."

"I didn't know I was walking loudly," Tally whispered back.

"More like this." I showed Tally how to take slow, even steps, like I do by the pond when I'm fishing.

Outside the band room, the lights were off. The building blended into the darkness. Except somebody must've forgotten to turn off a row of lights in the back.

We crept even closer. My heart beat an allegro tempo. Byrd could tell you, that meant fast.

"Let's climb in through a window," I said. "So nobody'll see us."

"I don't see a window."

"That's because your eyes are closed." This was Tally's idea, but now she was too freaked out to even open her eyes.

"Oh, right." She opened one eye then. "Which window should we go in?"

"Maybe the closest one. Slide to your left," I said, pointing even though she couldn't really see me.

So we tiptoed. Slowly. Until we stood directly beneath the window.

"We still can't get in, though," Tally said. "It's too high. Now what?"

Think, think, think. "I got it! Stand on my shoulders. I've seen that in a million movies."

"Not happening," Tally said. "I've seen it too, and it never ends well."

I glanced around then. "Let's grab those flower pots by the door and stand on 'em."

"But there are flowers growing in them. You don't want to kill those petunias, do you?"

"I think they're already dead." The purple blooms were completely wilted. But no, we couldn't finish 'em off. "Any other ideas?"

"Yeah," Tally said. "Duck! Somebody's coming!"

I looked up to see a flashlight beam scanning each side of the path to the band room.

"Who's there?" A voice boomed.

"It's Byrd," Tally whispered. "We're so busted."

Not yet. Not if Byrd didn't know it was us. I disguised my voice and did this awesome howling impression to make Byrd think it was just a stray cat roaming around. But he didn't fall for it.

"Zac," he said. "Is that you?" His flashlight's beam searched the shadows.

Tally flipped out. "Give it up, Zac! He knows."

"Is Tally with you?"

"Yes, sir," I said, holding up one hand to block the glare of light from my eyes.

"What on earth are you two doing out here?" Mr. Byrd started toward us. "You're supposed to be at the amphitheater watching *The Galaxy's Greatest Composers* with the other campers."

"Well, uh, see . . . ," I began.

Then there was a rustling sound on the other side of the band room.

"What was that?" Tally asked.

"Hey, I probably called up a cat. I've done it before."

"I don't think so," Mr. Byrd said, shining his flashlight in that direction. "Get behind me."

We followed him around the corner. Byrd shined his light in every bush.

"I don't see anything," Tally said.

I didn't either. But then we got to this one bush that looked different. Its branches were all flattened out in the middle.

Byrd crept over and aimed his flashlight at it.

"Hey, it's black," I said.

"Be careful, Zac. It could have rabies," Mr. Byrd warned.

I leaned in for a closer look. Real slow. Then I started laughing.

"Please, this is no time for clowning around," Mr. Byrd said.

"I'm sorry, sir." I reached into the bush. "But I've never heard of a sax case with rabies."

Even in the dark, I saw Byrd scratch his balding head. "A sax in the bushes," he said. "Why?"

"I dunno," I said.

Tally leaned in to read a tag on the handle. "Property of Jordan Dillihay."

Then I said, "Look! The cellar door is open."

Byrd flashed his light closer to the band room.

I eased over toward the door. "Shine your light down here, sir."

When he did, I went down the concrete steps leading into the cellar.

"Do you see anything, Zac?" Mr. Byrd asked.

"You won't believe this!" I climbed out, carrying another sax case. "It's mine! And there's more."

Byrd took the envelope I handed him and shined his flashlight on it. "Our sheet music," he said. Then he looked at me. "Innocent, huh?"

"Hey, I told you I didn't do it," I said.

"You certainly did," Mr. Byrd said.

Then Tally said, "I hear something else."

"Whoever did this is still in the band room," Mr. Byrd said. "And we're about to find out who it is."

Chapter 10

SOUND OFF!

"Who's in here?" Mr. Byrd asked sternly.

Nobody answered.

Then Byrd flipped the light switch off and on, off and on.

"Whoa! What's going on?"

Nate. *I knew it!*

"That's what I'd like to know," Mr. Byrd said. "Why are you in the band room alone this late at night, Nate?"

"I forgot I'd volunteered to water the plants," he said.

"He's lying!" I said. "Did you see those petunias by the door? They're as dry as a cactus."

Nate shook his head. "That's because I didn't water them yet. Aubrey was supposed to help water the inside plants, and Ethan was supposed to help me water the ones outside."

"So where's Aubrey? And Ethan?" I asked.

Byrd looked at me. "Slow down, Zac. I'll ask the questions." Then he said to Nate, "Where are Aubrey and Ethan?"

"Ethan never showed up," Nate said. "And Aubrey was here a few minutes ago when I went in the bathroom to fill up the watering can. Then I heard a noise over by the lockers and you started flicking the lights."

So we all went over to the lockers.

"Somebody left the window up," Nate said, reaching to close it.

Byrd stopped him. "Not yet. I see the screen's missing." He leaned out the window and shined his flashlight to the ground below. "Guess what's beneath this window?"

"The bush where we found the sax case?" I asked.

"Exactly!" Mr. Byrd said.

Ethan came rushing in then. "Sorry I'm late, Nate," he said. "I couldn't stop watching that movie about those old composer dudes. They were pretty cool."

"No problem," Nate said. Then he asked, "But what sax case are you talking about, Wiles?"

"I think you know," I said. "It belongs to some kid named Jordan." I guess Nate hadn't even noticed the case in my hand, so I held it up. "We found other cases in the cellar, too. One was mine."

"And our band's missing sheet music," Tally chimed in.

"Do you know anything about this, Nate?" Mr. Byrd asked.

"I'd like to hear Nate's answer, too."

We whirled around.

Mrs. Hendrix stood in the doorway. Aubrey was with her, and I could have sworn she looked guilty. That was a surprise.

"I think you all have some explaining to do." Mrs. Hendrix's high heels clicked across the floor toward us.

Nate opened his mouth, but Aubrey was the one who started talking.

"It was me." She stared at her sneakers. "I wanted our band to win Sound Off really bad. I took their sheet music to make them lose points."

"And my sax?" I asked.

"That too," she continued. "One day in the band room, you said the judges told you that you had a shot at the all-stars band. But I wanted my cousin to win it."

"Your cousin?" I asked.

"Yep." Aubrey nodded. "Nate."

Wow. I thought Nate took our sheet music and my sax. And I thought he was Aubrey's boyfriend. Turns out, I'm a rotten detective.

"But why did you take the other instruments?" Mrs. Hendrix asked.

"Because I wanted everyone to think Zac was the one doing it. So he'd get in trouble," Aubrey admitted.

"She framed me," I said. "I want a lawyer!"

"Zac." Mr. Byrd shook his head.

Mrs. Hendrix put one hand on Aubrey's shoulder and one on Nate's. "I'm disappointed in both of you."

Nate hadn't said much, but he did then. "I promise, I didn't know anything about any of this."

"He didn't!" Aubrey said. "Neither did Ethan. They volunteered to do stuff, so I helped them. But when they weren't looking, I took the sheet music. And I tossed the sax cases out the window until I could hide them in the cellar later."

"Oh, Aubrey," Mrs. Hendrix said. "I can't believe you'd do something like this."

"Me either!" I said.

"Zac." Mr. Byrd put a finger to his lips to shush me, but I couldn't stop.

"Hey, I'm serious," I said. "I didn't think it was Aubrey. I thought it was Nate the whole time." I looked at him. "I'm sorry I accused you, dude."

"I guess it did sort of look like I was the one doing it, especially when I was a jerk sometimes," Nate said.

I grinned. "Errr. Make that most of the time."

"Yeah, sorry about that." Nate smiled, too. "I was just goofing around. Sometimes I go a little too far, I guess."

Hey, I got that. Same thing happens to me sometimes, too.

"Well," Mrs. Hendrix began, "I'm glad you finally realize that, Nate. And Aubrey, I hope you realize you face serious consequences."

"One more," I said. "I wanna beat Nate."

It was our last day of camp. Some of the kids from our band and some other bands, too, were goofing off. We were stacking up instrument cases and then jumping over them. Whoever cleared them, without knocking them over, was the winner.

So far, that was Nate. When Nate wasn't practicing with the all-stars band, he and Ethan hung out with me. Not Aubrey, though. She went home early. That was part of the consequences her band director had told her about for hiding everyone's stuff.

"Zac! Knock it off!" Mr. Byrd said then, clapping his hands. "Let's go. It's time for the Sound Off winner to be officially announced."

I ran over to Byrd, and Nate started laughing. "You look like twins."

"Aloha!" I joked. Byrd wore a Hawaiian shirt with starfish all over it. And since Nate's band had the most points and won Sound Off, that meant I lost the bet Nate had made with me.

Byrd wasn't happy when I told him about the bet and asked to borrow his sea horse shirt. And even though the whole thing was Nate's idea, Byrd made me promise not to do it again. "Band is no place for bets," he'd said.

But he also said he was glad that I kept my end of the bargain, especially since we'd probably only lost because of all the stuff Aubrey did to cost us points.

When everyone was seated at the amphitheater, the frowny-face judge went up onstage.

"Good evening," she said. "This year, the band with the most points and our Sound Off winner is Morrison Junior High." She looked out into the crowd. "Mrs. Hendrix, please come up and accept this award on behalf of your band."

Everyone clapped and cheered when Mrs. Hendrix took the trophy.

"Thank you," Mrs. Hendrix said. "But due to some controversial events, our band doesn't feel like we fairly earned this award. I'm sorry, but we cannot accept it." She handed back the trophy to the frowny-face judge. "Please give it to the band that rightfully earned it."

The frowny-face judge nodded and gathered on the side of the stage with the other judges. When she came back to center stage a few minutes later, she said, "This is unusual. But considering the week's events, we are proud to give this award to Benton Bluff Junior High." She held up the trophy. "Mr. Byrd, will you please accept your award?"

Byrd went up onstage. "Thank you, judges. And thank you, Mrs. Hendrix," he spoke into the mic. "It's been a bizarre week, to say the least. But I'm honored to accept this award. And I'm even more honored to direct an extraordinary group of kids." He motioned for us to come up onstage. "Come accept your award, Benton Bluff band. You've earned it."

We all ran up to join Byrd onstage.

"Cool! I can see myself in this thing!" Sherman checked out his reflection in our trophy.

Tally reached for it. "Lemme see!" Then she and Baylor made kissy faces at themselves.

"It's nice. But hey, it was even nicer when Byrd finally admitted the truth." I smiled. "We're extraordinary!"

"He meant everybody but you, Zac," Davis joked.

"Nah, he meant me, too," I said. "Right, Mr. Byrd?"

He laughed then. "Even you, Zac."

"Back at you, sir."